Turn the page for a sneak preview of the
next Dr. Siri Paiboun investigation

Thirty-Three Teeth

The neon hammer and sickle buzzed and flickered into life over the night club of the Lan Xang Hotel. The sun had plummeted mauvely into Thailand across the Mekhong River, and the hotel waitresses were lighting the little lamps that turned the simple sky-blue room into a mysterious nighttime cavern.

In an hour, a large Vietnamese delegation would be offered diversion there by members of the Lao People's Revolutionary Party Politburo. They'd be made to watch poor country boys in fur hats do a Lao falling-over version of cossack dancing. They'd be forced to suck semi-fermented rice whiskey from large tubs through long straws until they were dizzy. They'd finally be coerced into embarrassing dances with solid girls in ankle-length skirts and crusty makeup.

And, assuming they survived these delights, they'd be allowed to return to their rooms to sleep. Next day, with heads heavy as pressed rubber, they'd sign their names to documents laying the foundations for the forthcoming Lao/Vietnam Treaty of Friendship, and they probably wouldn't remember very much about it.

But that was all to come. The understaffed hotel day shift had been replaced by an understaffed night crew. The sweating receptionist was ironing a shirt in the glass office behind her desk. The chambermaid was running a bowl of rice porridge up to a sick guest on the third floor.

Outside, an old guard, in a jacket so large it reached his knees, was locking the back gate that opened onto Sethathirat Road. At night, the gate kept out dogs and the occasional traveler tempted to come into the garden in search of respite from the cruel hot-season nights. An eight-foot wall protected the place as if it were something more special than it was.

Leaves floated in a greasy swimming pool. Obedient flowers stood in well-spaced regiments, better watered than any of the households outside along the street. And then there were the cages. They were solid concrete, so squat that a tall man would have to stoop to see inside. Two were empty. They housed only the spirits of animals temporarily imprisoned there: a monkey replaced by a deer, a peacock taking over the sentence of a wild dog.

But in the grim shadows of the third cage, something wheezed. It moved seldom, only to scratch lethargically at its dry skin. The unchristened black mountain bear was hosed down along with the bougainvilleas and given scraps from the kitchen from time to time. Its fur was patchy and dull, like a carpet in a well-trodden passage. Buddha only knew how the creature had survived for so long in its cramped jail, and the Lord had been banished from the socialist republic some fifteen months hence.

People came in the early evening and at weekends to stand in front of the cage and stare at her. She stared back, although her glazed bloodshot eyes could no longer make out details of the mocking faces. Children laughed and pointed. Brave fathers poked sticks in through the bars, but the black mountain bear no longer appeared to give a damn.

They naturally blamed the old guard the next day. "Too much rice whiskey," they said. "Slack," they said. The guard denied it, of course. He swore he'd relocked the cage door. He'd thrown the leftovers from the Vietnamese banquet into the animal's bowl and locked the cage. He was sure of it. He swore the beast was still in there when he did his rounds at four. He swore he had no idea how it could have gotten out, or where it could have gone. But they sacked him anyway.

After a panicked search of the grounds and the hotel buildings, the manager declared to his staff that the place was safe and it was a problem now for the police. In fact, he didn't think it would be wise to mention the escape to his guests at all. As far as he was concerned, the problem was over.

But for Vientiane, it had barely started.

Tomb Sweet Tomb

The sun baked everything in the new suburb. Comrade Civilai stepped from the hot black limousine and, without locking the doors, walked up to the concrete mausoleum where they'd put Dr. Siri. The gate and the front door were open, and he could see clear through to the small yard at the back. There was no furniture to interrupt the view.

He kicked off his Sunday sandals and walked into the front room. It was as if the builders and decorators had just left. The walls were still virgin Wattay light-blue, to match the swimming-pool-colored Wattay airport. They were unencumbered by pictures or posters or photographs of heroes of the revolution. No French plaster ducks flew in formation. No clock ticked. If he didn't know Siri had lived here for a month, he would have guessed this to be a vacant house.

On his way to the back, he passed a small room where piles of clothes told him he was nearing a primitive life form. In the back yard, he discovered it. Dr. Siri Paiboun, reluctant national coroner, confused psychic, disheartened communist, swung gently on a hammock strung between two jackfruit saplings. A larger man would have brought them both down.

In his shadow, Saloop, rescued street dog and lifesaver, drooled onto the hot earth. He looked up with one eye, decided Civilai was too old and bald to be a threat, and returned to his dream.

A month earlier, the yard had been dirt and debris. Today it was a jungle. Siri had gone to great pains to recreate the environment in which he'd spent the latter forty of his seventy-two years. For the past four weekends, he and his trusted morgue colleagues had set off into the outer suburbs and denuded them unashamedly. They'd transported a variety of trees and shrubs back to this humble bunker—the Party's thanks for his services.

"I do hope I'm not disturbing you," Civilai said, knowing full well how disturbing he was being. Siri's eerie green eyes opened slowly to see his best friend leaning over him.

"Ah, boy. Just put the iced lime juice on the table there and get back to the servants' quarters post-haste."

Civilai was two days older than the doctor. Both born in the year of the rabbit, they showed its characteristic industry and guile. Yet neither had exhibited its lustiness: they'd married their first loves and been totally faithful. They were of a rare breed of rabbit in Laos.

"So, this is how the bourgeois medical profession spends its Sundays. Shouldn't you be out digging ditches for the republic?" He sat back on the wooden cot on the small veranda.

"I'm a frail old man, brother. A day of physical labor could very well put me on the slab. I doubt I have a month left to live as it is. That's why your politburo buddies should be searching high and low for a coroner to replace me now."

There was nothing frail about Dr. Siri. He was so far from the black archers of death, he wouldn't be hearing their arrows thumping into the dry earth for many years to come. His short, solid body still scurried hither and thither like a curious river rat. Younger men were hard-pressed to keep his pace.

His mind, resplendent with its newly honed skills, had become even keener of late. He'd always been a logical man; but in the last five months, he'd acquired the type of knowledge that isn't given out in universities. For reasons he was still trying to fathom, he'd been delegated Laos's honorary consul to the spirit world.

This new posting proved ideally suited to his job as the head and only coroner of the Lao People's Democratic Republic. He still hadn't been able to control the visits from his spirit clients or find a way to ask specific questions of them, but they came to him regularly with clues. What he lacked in experience (he'd only been a coroner for a year), he could often make up for by communing with the dead. His three-dimensional mind had acquired a fourth dimension.

"You know we could never replace you, Little Brother. You're a legend," Civilai replied.

"A legend?" Siri slid up the hammock to a sitting position. "Isn't a legend something that's long-winded and not widely believed?"

"You've got it."

"Hot, isn't it?"

"Damned hot."

This was the hot-season anthem that could be heard *ad infinitum* around the capital. It had been a particularly hot year so far, so it got even more repetition than usual.

For the first time, Siri noticed the cloth bag that Civilai held on his lap. "You bring me something?"

"Nothing you'd be interested in."

"Let me be the judge of that."

"The Soviets have been courting us. They want permission to build a satellite dish to spy on the Yanks. While we think about it, they pepper us with these little incentives." He teased the cap of a bottle from his bag.

"Vodka?"

"Moskovskaya; best you can get. But I don't suppose you're thirsty."

Siri was off the hammock and rattling around in the kitchen for a second glass before the word *thirsty* had left Civilai's lips.

The late morning had become late afternoon.

"I don't know how the Russians can strink-this-duff." Civilai's slurring turned the comment into one long word.

"Me, too. No wonder the women are hairier than the women."

"Men."

"Where?"

So had the conversation deteriorated. There were two modest glassfuls left in the bottom of the bottle. The friends sat side by side on the long, uncomfortable wooden cot. The garden wasn't moving at all, but they swayed like survivors in a lifeboat. Civilai looked up at a rolled mosquito net tied above their heads.

"You sleep out here, Li'l Brother?"

Siri shook his head from side to side. "Yes."

"What's the point of having a house?"

"That's it. That's the very something I asked Judge Haeng. But he wouldn't let me have the garden without it. He said—Siri put on the whiny high-pitched accent of his young superior—'We are senior members of the party, Comrade Siri. As such, we have to lead by example. Sleeping in trees should remain the exclusive domain of the primates.' I was surprised he knew what a primate was."

"What have you got against houses?"

"Houses I have not a nothing against. But this isn't a house. A house is an airy wooden thing on slits that—"

"Stilts."

"I said that. On slits, that creaks when you walk around. It sways in heavy winds and leaks in the rainy season. This? This is a sarcahoph . . . a . . . a saroph . . . sarpho . . . sarcophagus."

"Well said."

"What is this regime's fixation on concrete?"

"Sustainability. This house will still be here in a thousand years, after ten generations of your wooden houses have fallen down. Remember the three little pigs."

"That's it. It's a sty."

"It's not."

"Then it's a tomb. I feel entombed. It's so morbid in there."

"How can you, of all people, complain about morbidity?"

"I'm a coroner. Not a corpse."

Civilai laughed and leaned back against the wall. "How are your ghostly friends, by the way?"

Siri looked at him to see whether he was about to make fun of his spiritual connections—as he always did.

"There hasn't been a lot of activity since the floating Vietnamese last November. But then again, we haven't had too many mysteries lately."

"They only come out in times of confusion?"

"No. They're around all the time. They all make an appearance, but they don't necessessarily do anything. I get an old lady sitting opposite me in the office late—he hiccuped—excuse me, at night. She just sits there. I keep waiting for her to do something, flash me a tit or some such, but she just sits, chewing betel, staring at me."

"You know, Siri, sometimes you scare the daylights out of me." Civilai leaned over and poured the remains of the Soviet bribe into their chipped glasses. "We should finish this up before it eats through the bottom of the bottle."

"A toast to the illustrious Union of Sovalist Republicists."

"I don't think you need any more."

They quaffed the dregs and Siri got unsteadily to his feet.

"Thank God that's over. Now we can have some deluscious coffee."

The late afternoon was becoming evening.

The shadows from the instant jungle had fallen across the two pickled patriots and were climbing the concrete wall behind them. The chewy coffee was shocking them out of their Sunday stupors. Civilai made one last attempt to encourage his friend to feel at home.

"I think this place is quite charming."

"Then I'll move in with your wife and you can live here."

"Let me think about that."

"It was supposed to be a reward, but it's more like punishment, Older Brother. I've got busybody Miss Vong on one side of me and some corrupt local official from Oudom Xay on the other."

"Surely you could shout that a little bit louder."

Siri ignored him. "I've got a goddamned loudspeaker blaring out diatribes against the non-communist world right there at the corner of the street from five A. goddamned M. I couldn't be any more unhappy."

"All you need here is a good woman to turn it into a home. I don't suppose you've—"

"Don't."

"I was only wondering if you'd—"

"Don't."

"—contacted her. That's all."

"No. And I won't. Don't ask again."

"Seems silly to me."

Siri sulked for a moment or two. There had only been one woman, one date, since Boua had died. It was a disaster of a date. Siri knew Lah was a woman he could love. The feeling was returned. Auntie Lah had custom-made baguettes for him at her cart opposite Mahosot Hospital from the first week he arrived there. They joked, they flirted, and she made no secret of the fact she liked him.

Once Boua, his only love, his long-departed wife, had given her postmortem permission, he went at that new romance like a teenager. On the night of the fateful date when he first saw Lah waiting there, glamorous and preening like a *Likay* queen, the butterflies in his belly had almost lifted him from the seat of his motorbike.

She ran over on her unfamiliar heels and sniffed the air at his cheek. He felt the brush of her lips, and parts of him that had been in hibernation for many years began to stir. It was all marvelously portentous. He was at the precipice overlooking what he knew could be a wonderful final cycle to his life.

He was about to leap when she handed him the gift. It was beautifully wrapped and expensively heavy. She said it was something she'd found at the morning market. She said it was as if it had spoken to her. She believed it could stymie his run of bad luck. He opened the box, and all his hope caved in like some badly built temple stupa.

In the cardboard coffin lay a black amulet eroded by decades of hopeful fingers. It was attached to a fraying leather thong. Siri knew it well.

Lah smiled, expecting a smile in return from her dashing beau. But, instead, the expression on his face frightened her. His unkempt white eyebrows gathered at the center of a furrowed brow. He shook his head slowly and asked "How could you do this?"

"Wha—?"

Siri had sped off on his motorcycle clutching the amulet in his left hand, without saying another word. She watched him go with her cherry-red bottom lip hanging open. Of course she had no idea what she'd done. She thought she was showing him a kindness. She thought she was giving him a token of her affection. But it had turned out to be doom. She never saw him again and never understood why.

Siri had ridden to the Mekhong at its deepest point and hurled the amulet far out into the murky brown water. There were no coincidences any more in his life. That, he knew. Everything was inked on some sacred parchment. Malevolent spirits were in pursuit of him. The previous year at an exorcism in Khamuan, he'd been given this very amulet, an antique black stone, to ward off the evil spirits of the forest; the *Phibob*. But it had turned out to be a trick. The stone was actually a spiritual lintel that opened a gateway from their world to his. He'd been lucky to survive their attack. Now they wanted revenge on him. Lah had been selected to deliver this omen, and she was in danger as a result. It was clear that she could never be a part of his life. No matter how strongly he felt attracted to her, it was impossible.

Of course, Civilai said that was all a pile of buffalo dung. He said when the chance of a little over-seventy nooky presented itself, one shouldn't read too much into coincidence. "At our age, my little brother, these opportunities don't come along every day."

"It wasn't a coincidence. I sent those spirits packing, and in so doing I saved the soldiers that were cutting down their trees. They weren't happy about that. But I tell you, that stone had been destroyed."

"Did you see that happen with your own eyes?"

"Yes. Well, not with my own eyes. But I saw the dust before the Hmong took it out to the forest."

"Then you can't be sure it came from the stone. Mystery one solved."

"So how did it get here, to Vientiane? How did it get to the market? And of all the people who could have bought it, why Lah?"

"I'm an elder statesman with a not-inconsequential intellect. I can solve many of the conundrums that arise from the day-to-day running of a little country in the southeast of Asia. But I have a one-mystery-a-day quota," Civilai said. "Release me now. I have to get home to my dear wife. Remind me where my car is."

"You think you should drive?"

"Certainly. What is there to hit?"

Siri nodded and escorted him to the door. Civilai was right. On a Sunday afternoon in March, Vientiane had the atmosphere of a town in the talons of a deadly plague. A motorcyclist might brave the late-afternoon heat. A dog might lie on the concrete paving stones to burn off the fleas. But most folks were at home, waiting for the sun to go down.

At dusk, the girls would two-up on bicycles and ride slowly along Fangoum Road, catching some small breeze from the river and advertising their availability to boys two-upping in the opposite direction. They would still be mopping their sweating brows with their mothers' large pink handkerchiefs until long after nightfall.

Farewell the Diarrhetic

Old Auntie See lived in a shed behind a peeling white French colonial mansion that now housed five families. For a living, she bought fruit at the morning market, cut it into colorful slices, and sold it from a card table beside her back gate.

Business was never too brisk, since money for luxuries had become scarcer. As a result, her main diet was overly ripe fruit, which saw her spending much of her nights in the tin latrine behind the shed.

On that particular Sunday night, whilst engaged in her dribbly business, she thought she heard a growl. There were footsteps through the undergrowth of her uncared-for garden. They were too heavy to be those of a dog, but somehow too zigzag and rambling to be those of a person. She called out anyway: "Can't a woman have a shit in peace any more?"

There was no answer. The noises stopped. And after a few more minutes she forgot all about them. Diarrhea, in its most vindictive state, can erase even thoughts of terror.

Some twenty minutes later, she groaned and rearranged her long cotton *phasin* around her waist. She stepped through the corrugated tin door, and before she could stoop to wash her hands in the paint can basin, that thing was on her. She had no time to scream—to run—or even to turn her head to see what was biting into the back of her neck. With one swipe of its powerful arm, she was dead.

Two Dead Men on a Bicycle

Siri arrived at the hospital on Monday morning with a vodka hammer beating and a vodka sickle scything through his head. He guessed he couldn't have a worse hangover if he'd drunk the formaline straight from the sample bottles. Every step from the motorcycle park to the morgue jarred new agony into his brain. There was no question in his mind that the Soviet Union was doomed.

He walked beneath the French MORGUE sign, carefully wiped his feet on the American WELCOME mat, and stepped inside the cool dark single-story building. He immediately sensed one or two presences, but was far too vodka'd to acknowledge them. They could wait.

He walked into his office, whose blue walls had been thoroughly whitewashed again and again until they were gray. Anything that wasn't blue suited Siri just fine. Nurse Dtui was sitting at her desk.

"Morning, Comrade Siri," she said, flashing her small, neat teeth but not stirring her large, untidy body.

"Good morning, Dtui."

Those first words of the day came out like a gravel driveway.

"Oh-ho. Have a bit of a session last night, did we?"

"A cultural experiment."

He flopped into his chair, and his head turned to percussion. He buried it in his hands.

"Looks like the experiment failed."

"No, my faithful assistant. Never assume that negative experiences teach you less than positive ones. I have it filed away that in the future, no matter how free, no matter how fascinating the squiggles on the bottle, I shall avoid Russian vodka as if it were a musty elephant."

Dtui stood. Her uniform was bleached white and stretched across her large frame like butcher's paper around a hock of pork.

"What you need is some of my ma's herbal brew."

"Oh, no. Don't say it. Haven't I suffered enough?"

"Don't go away."

She headed for the door.

"Where's our other soldier?"

"He's in the examination room getting the new guests ready." She stopped in the doorway. "You'll like this one: two men dead on a bicycle in the middle of the street. No spare seat or luggage rack. They were going around Nam Poo fountain in the middle of town. Nothing there could have been going fast enough to hit them. They were found on top of the bike. No blood. This looks like a job for . . . dah-dah-da-dah."

"Dtui?"

". . . Super Spirit Doc."

She giggled and walked out of the office. Siri groaned. The last thing he wanted on that particular morning was to cut anyone up. He especially didn't want anything inexplicable to trouble his hurting head.

Dtui was fumbling in the back of the freezer for the corked bottle that held her mother's secret brew. Although there was a hospital ban on using the morgue freezers for personal perishables, her ma's brew looked enough like body waste to fool the most pedantic inspector. It was an evil Macbethian mix of bizarre ingredients that tasted horrible but cured just about anything.

"Wha . . . wha . . . what's that for, Dtui?" Mr. Geung was laying out the second cyclist on the spare aluminum table. Geung was a good-looking man in his forties with pronounced Down-Syndrome features and jet-black hair greased on either side of a crooked center parting. When he asked a question, he had the habit of rocking slightly where he stood. Judge Haeng at the Department of Justice, which oversaw the work of Siri and his team, was lobbying for the removal of the "moron," but Geung's condition was neither serious nor disruptive to his work. Although he often became anxious about anomalies outside the regimented pattern of his days, he was a morgue assistant par excellence. He'd been trained with infinite patience by Siri's predecessor and knew the procedures better than Dtui or Siri himself. He was strong and reliable, and he wielded a mean hacksaw.

"The boss has got himself a hangover," Dtui said.

Geung snorted a laugh. "Al . . . alcohol is the elixir of the d . . . devil."

"Was that another one of your father's wisdoms?"

"No. Comrade Dr. Siri . . . ss . . . said it when we cut open the drunk fellow on January first."

That was one other thing. You didn't want to say anything you'd live to regret when Mr. Geung was around. He didn't forget much.

The autopsy followed the standard pattern they'd settled into. Siri was beginning to sit back and let Dtui give the commentary while he took notes. She was learning the trade and hoped to be sent to the Eastern Bloc on a scholarship. Her eyes were keen, and she often noticed things that Siri had missed. The only setback to this new system was that nobody could read Siri's notes afterward. Not even Siri.

As the two bodies in the morgue hadn't been reported as missing, they would temporarily be known as Man A and Man B.

They were an ill-matched pair. Man A was neatly dressed in a white shirt. He had on an old but quite costly wristwatch, wore permanent-press slacks, and had soft, uncallused hands which suggested he wasn't used to manual labor. But, as Siri and Dtui both noticed, the most remarkable thing about him was that he was wearing socks. The March temperatures were already hitting 107 degrees. Even in those few offices where ancient French air conditioners waged battle with the heat, the best they could ever achieve was "tepid." It was *never* so cold you'd need to wear socks.

No, these socks suggested that the poor man had no choice. Since he had become coroner, Siri had been under pressure to wear the black vinyl shoes provided by the Party. It was an example of what he termed the new "shoe over substance" policy. So far, he'd been able to use his seniority and his stubborn streak to remain in his brown leather sandals. But he knew that if he were finally compressed into those toe-torturers, he certainly would have to wear socks also.

Dtui spoke his thought. "I'd say he's government."

"The socks?"

"The fingers."

She was constantly surprising him. Siri went over and held up Mr. A's hand. All the fingertips were purple: triplicate syndrome.

It was Civilai who'd coined the phrase to describe the peculiar mauve "bruising" so common in socialist bureaucracies. They were bogged down in paperwork, as there had to be copies for every department. This called into play that miracle of modern office timesaving: carbon paper.

Like its shoes and its hair dye, Laos got its carbon paper from China. So most officials that used it found more ink on themselves than on the paper. Mr. A had thumbed his share of carbon sheets.

They stripped him, bagged and labeled his clothes, and took

their allotted four color photographs of his outside. Siri noted that no shoes had arrived with the body. There was a thin trail of congealed blood at the corner of the mouth and severe bruising to the chest and abdomen.

Before beginning an internal examination, Siri decided to prepare Mr. B for the chop also. This would ultimately save time and allow them to make comparisons of their respective injuries. Siri ignored Dtui's comment that "This is how they do it at the abattoir," and asked her to voice her observations about Mr. B.

She noted that he was certainly from a different end of town than Mr. A. His clothes were threadbare and quite dirty. His hands were rough and covered in scabs of short nicks as if he'd been cut often.

"So, the question remains," Siri pondered, almost to himself, ". . . what were two men from very different backgrounds doing sharing a bicycle at two in the morning?"

"Perhaps," Dtui suggested, "this one was the chauffeur and he was taking his master home."

Geung let out one of his farmyard laughs.

"Or perhaps they weren't on the bicycle at all." Siri glared. "I'm starting to think the fact they were found with the bike was a coincidence."

"So, how did they get there?"

"Oh, I don't know everything, Miss Dtui. Perhaps the old chap ran into the government fellow when he was crossing the road."

"Yeah? And how fast would he have been pedaling to kill the pair of them?"

"Or, alternatively, the government fellow was riding a motorbike and hit the old boy."

"And . . . ?"

"And someone ran off with the motorbike."

"I suppose I could buy that one."

"Did the police bring in the bicycle, Mr. Geung?"

"It's round the b . . . round the b . . . the back."

"Good. We can take a look at it later."

They stripped Mr. B. Apart from his obviously broken neck and the massive bruising associated with vertebral artery trauma, there were no recent abrasions or visible marks on him. They finished up the film and laid him out. There the two corpses reclined on either side of the room, like temple step ornaments.

The dual autopsy took exactly two hours. Mr. A had hemorrhaging around the chest cavity and livor mortis around the main artery common in victims of high-speed collisions, so the motorcycle theory still held. Some trauma had also been sufficiently violent to rupture his testicles. From these initial examinations, Siri surmised that the broken neck had killed Mr. B, and the internal bleeding Mr. A. But there were other tests to do.

Mr. Geung cut through the tough crania with his old hacksaw, and Siri tied cotton around the brains in order to suspend them in Formalin for two or three days until they were set firm enough to cut into.

Dtui took samples of the stomach contents and blood. As they had no lab, there were only limited secrets these could disclose. The next day, Siri would take a ride over to the Lycée Vientiane, where he would coerce Teacher Oum into using the last of her science lab chemicals on color tests.

Somewhere out at the customs shed, a crate of school chemicals, kindly donated by the high-school cooperative in Vladivostok, had sat for three months collecting paperwork. Even being the national coroner didn't carry any weight in pushing that old bureaucratic bus up the hill to socialist nirvana.

Dtui, Geung, and Siri sat on their haunches around the bicycle. The rusty thing that had survived many battles would never be ridden again.

"Now, what do you suppose could cause something like this?" Siri asked of no one in particular. The frame supporting the chain was buckled and almost touching the ground. The handlebars leaned back, the seat forward.

"It looks like I sat on it," Dtui said, causing a laughing fit in Mr. Geung that took a good deal of back-slapping to arrest.

"No," Siri said at last. "It would take half a dozen Dtuis to do this. But I think I know what could. What side of the fountain were they found on?"

"Ministry side."

"I think we'd better go and take a look, don't you?"

"Is your head up to it?"

"Ah, Dtui. There's nothing like the dissection of corpses and a dollop of your ma's brew to cure a hangover."

The Ministry of Sport, Information and Culture currently and unofficially occupied a seven-story building that overlooked the non-spouting fountain at Nam Poo Square. Given the shape of things in Laos, the square was, naturally, a circle. It was surrounded by quaint and largely neglected two-storied buildings that wouldn't have felt out of place in a small southern French village. It was a sleepy square where old ladies dried white spring-roll wrappings on mesh tables and crazy Rajid the Indian walked slow laps around the dull concrete fountain.

Although the Lao weren't yet conceited enough to refer to most of their government departments as anything more grand, Vientiane people had begun to call the incongruous building that housed the sports department "The Ministry." It was probably the size of the place, rather than its grandeur, that impressed them. The old French Cultural Center had all the architectural class of a two-star hotel in a seaside resort. The Sport, Information and Culture people rattled around inside its large rooms like a destitute woman's beads in a once-full jewelry box.

Mr. Geung had stayed back at the morgue to keep an eye on the guests. Dtui, on her first investigative mission away from the hospital, stood in the middle of the road beside the angels chalked there on the asphalt. Siri was twelve meters away, with his back against the wall of The Ministry. He painted an imaginary arc with his eyebrows from the point where Dtui stood up to the top ledge of the building above him. He shook his head and walked over to the nurse.

"No good?" She asked.

"Well, it isn't impossible, but . . . I don't know. He either took one almighty running jump, or he was tossed. And if someone had thrown him, we would have found marks on his arms or legs. But we didn't."

"You don't think he might have—"

A Vespa scooter came putt-ing around the fountain, causing Siri to leap from its path into the unsuspecting arms of Dtui.

"Dr. Siri. You romantic old thing, you."

Embarrassed, he untangled himself from her embrace. The scooter stopped a few meters further on, and the rider, a trim attractive man in his forties, looked back and laughed. Inspector Phosy got down, hoisted the silly vehicle onto its stand, and hurried back with a handshake at the ready. Siri grabbed the hand, and the two men patted each other's backs as they embraced.

"Hot, isn't it?"

"Damned hot."

"How's my favorite policeman?"

"Dr. Siri. I thought you were dead."

"Don't you be so sure I'm not." They broke apart, and Siri looked along the street. "That's a very impressive cop bike you have. Lilac's the crime-suppression color of the year, I hear."

"Be kind, Comrade. These are hard times. We have to take what we can get." He looked over Siri's shoulder. "Good health, Dtui. You haven't lost any weight."

"And you're no better looking."

She shook his hand warmly.

"So," Siri asked. "How did you get this case?"

"They put me on anything with the word 'government' attached to it. As soon as Dtui called and suggested the victim could be a government official, they took me out of the cupboard. How hard do you think this is going to be? Was it a suicide?"

"I don't know. It's odd. Unless he was trying to fly, I don't see why he wouldn't just drop from the roof. He'd be just as dead without trying to reach the fountain."

"All right, then. Let's see if we can get any information from the information department."

They walked together through the elegant wooden doors and found themselves in a foyer containing nothing but a table. On the table was a small, hand-written sign that said ALL INQUIRIES UPSTAIRS.

Their footsteps echoed up the teak staircase. They noted how stuffy the place felt. Despite the heat, most of the windows hadn't been opened since the Americans left. (French culture had briefly been supplanted there by American language classes before the building's current manifestation.) The only culture not in evidence was Lao. Or perhaps it was.

On the second floor, they passed two rooms empty of furniture and life. The third door was slightly ajar, and through the gap they could see two metal cabinets, an uneven shelf with all its books resting at the low end, and a desk with a man on it.

He slept in his undershirt with a blissful expression on his young face. His ironed white shirt made a scarecrow over his chair. Although it was twenty minutes past one, and officially office hours, Phosy knocked politely and said "I'm sorry."

As the man didn't stir, he was about to knock a second time when Siri pushed past him into the room. The doctor was a remarkably patient man, but he had no time for incompetence in the government sector. He and Boua had fought for most of their lives to end corrupt systems and he had no intention of being part of one. In his most officious voice, he belted out: "Good God, man! What do you think you're doing? This is a government department, not a rest home. What if there was some sporting emergency or something?"

Phosy and Dtui raised their eyebrows at each other.

The man came out of his dream flailing, sending a stand of nicely sharpened pencils on a flight across the room. He leaped from the desktop and into his shoes. The visitors watched as he ran around the desk, gathered his shirt, and put it on. He was a plain-looking man with a naturally confused expression. He sat on the chair, fastened his shirt buttons, and, as if they hadn't witnessed the entire resurrection, asked his visitors, "May I help you?"

Phosy, smiling, handed him a mimeographed sheet with his photograph stapled to a top corner. This was his ID. The man scrutinized it with great care.

"Police?" he concluded.

"Very good. There was a death in front of The Ministry last night. Maybe early this morning. Are you missing anyone?"

"Now, that's hard to say."

"Why?"

"We're missing people all the time. Staff off in other provinces. People off sick. We haven't seen the head or deputy head for over a week."

"Isn't there some schedule? Some way to check who is supposed to be where?"

"Hmm. No."

"Where's the office that arranges all the trips?"

"Oh, right. That would be me."

"And you don't keep some kind of list?"

"It's a good idea, but nobody's ever asked before. You'd have to go from room to room and see who's missing."

So that's what they did. Siri was impressed that the department of information could provide so little of it. The search began on the second floor and worked its way up. The young man took them to rooms and introduced them to barely-stressed secretaries and average men whose jobs appeared to be to read newspapers, magazines, and novels.

Siri described the dead man at each office in turn, but soon realized that he could be talking about half the men who worked there. They all wore stay-press trousers and vinyl shoes, and were at varying stages of triplicate syndrome.

The administration rooms on the fifth floor were mostly empty, and the door leading to the top two floors was apparently locked. While the staff ran around looking for a key to open it, ever-resourceful Dtui noticed that there was already a key in the lock from the other side. They knocked and shouted for someone to come down and let them up, but when their banging was met by stony silence the worst was assumed.

"Who works up there?" Siri asked.

"Archives," said the young man. "It's like our history department. You know? Preservation and the like."

Siri wondered to himself how much priority the regime was placing on safeguarding the country's heritage, given that there weren't even funds available to station guards at the cultural sites. Anyone who fancied a coffee-table bust of the Buddha could just go and help himself.

After no more than two minutes on her knees, with the deft use of her watch pin and the careful placement of a newspaper beneath the door, Dtui was able to remove and retrieve the key on the other side of the door. Phosy looked on in admiration.

"You know? There are one or two unsolved burglary cases from the old regime. . ."

"Couldn't have been me, Officer. I wore gloves. Oops."

They reinserted the key and opened the door, and Phosy led the way up the staircase to the sixth and seventh floors, which were little more than a few rooms attached to the roof.

Siri sensed some unsettled force as he followed the others. He didn't feel confident enough of his instincts to warn anyone to be careful.

The main archive department was one large room on the seventh floor. It was in a terrible state. Pots were shattered and spread across the floor. Maps and stone rubbing sheets had been ripped from the walls. Beyond the mess, two things caught Phosy's eye. The large glass French windows were open, the glass smashed and the catch broken. Beyond them was a trajectory that would have taken a potential jumper swiftly to the chalk angel marks on the road beside the fountain. But he'd have had to take a run at it.

He also took note of the parallel shoes on the floor beside the overturned desk. With all the broken crockery around, it was unlikely the man would have taken them off before the jump. So the chaos had apparently not yet occurred. Phosy stuck his head out the window and looked either side. There was no way an assailant could have left the room via the window and escaped without a parachute. He turned back to see the others starting to clean up the mess.

"All right. Nobody touches anything till my people have had a chance to look around. Now, Mr. . . . . what's your name?"

"Santhi."

"Mr. Santhi. Who works in this office?"

"Mrs. Bounhieng. She's off having another baby. And Mr. Chansri. He's the director of the archives. And Mr. Khampet."

"And do either of those two gentlemen fit the description of the chap in the morgue?"

"Oh. Mr. Khampet. Definitely. Mr. Chansri's an older gentleman, and a little overweight."

"And where might we find the director of the archives?" Santhi shifted uneasily and looked at the ground. "Did you hear the question?"

"Yes."

"Well?"

"He could be at Tong Kankum market."

"I take it he isn't on ministry business."

"He sells fish."

"Right."

"I probably shouldn't have told you. But you understand. We don't get paid a lot here, so some of us supplement. . ."

"Mr. Santhi. I'm not a government inspector." Phosy looked across to see Siri on his haunches looking beneath the heavy wooden workbench. "What's that?"

"You see this?"

The detective walked across and looked under the bench.

"An old chest."

"No. It's a lot more than an old chest. Look. It has the royal seal."

Embossed onto a solid teak box, an improbable three-headed elephant stood on a podium like some circus freak at the That Luang Festival. It sheltered beneath a multi-tiered umbrella. Only time had removed its glitter. Siri lowered his voice. "The chest has a lot of energy, too. Whatever's in there is giving off a lot of aggression."

"Siri, you aren't having one of your supernatural moments?"

Very few people knew of the extent of Siri's mystic connections. In fact, only Civilai, Dtui, and Geung, in his own way, knew just how weird the doctor was. Siri had only recently become aware of his gifts himself. On the same visit to his birthplace in Khamuan when the *Phibob* had been roused, he'd been informed of something remarkable. In truth, he still didn't believe all the things he'd heard. According to the elders of one small village, Siri was the re-embodiment of Yeh Ming, a powerful Hmong shaman who had lived over a thousand years ago. Since the discovery, Siri had become aware of amazing powers that lurked somewhere deep inside him. As yet, he was unsure of how to use them, and in many ways they frightened the daylights out of him. He'd never directly informed Phosy of his unbidden gifts, but the policeman's instincts told him all he needed to know.

Siri reached out his hand toward the chest, and then withdrew it suddenly as if a shock had warned him off.

"I'd tell your people to be very careful of this, if I were you. Very careful."

Siri's dream that night didn't answer any questions for him. Mr. A, now positively identified as Khampet, was floating slowly down through the air toward Nam Poo fountain. He floated like a hawk but had a look of horror on his face. The ends of long staves of wood were nailed to his hands and feet. Another entered the back of his neck and appeared to go up into his head. But these didn't seem to worry him. He was more concerned about what was behind him, and whatever that was, it didn't appear in the dream shot. The occult cameraman wasn't giving anything away.

But just for a brief second, not long enough to be certain, Siri may have seen a line of witnesses on the roof above. They seemed happy—or perhaps *satisfied* would be a better description. In that brief second, he had a feeling they were old performers, the type that wore thick makeup and traditional Lao costumes. They may also have been applauding, but it's possible that Siri had been trying so hard to see something, he'd imagined the whole thing.

That's what he believed when he awoke. As was common after he'd had one of his dreams, he found himself in a state that may have been consciousness, or may have been a continuation of the dream. These were the scary moments when the visitors felt so real they could have been in the room with him.

It was quiet. The stars were still blurred by the heat rising from the hot earth, so he was certain he hadn't been asleep long. He was on the veranda behind his mausoleum. The mosquito net shimmied from a rare puff of summer breeze. It moved again. And again. It was swaying gently in time to some slow but regular stimulus.

Siri turned his head and looked into the darkness, and into the dull eyes of a bear. It was so close, its breath moved the net. It was close enough that Siri could see fresh blood at the corner of its mouth; close enough for him to smell the decay on its teeth.

It was sitting, watching the doctor. He felt its power over him. But Siri wasn't fearful. Yes, he believed this was unreal in some way, but he also had an instinct that the animal wasn't there to hurt him. The creature, its inspection over, rose painfully, turned, and walked off into the mobile jungle.

When Siri next awoke, it was certainly morning and the sun was threatening to rise over Miss Vong's well-scrubbed house. Before he could forget it, and before the government loudspeakers could begin their obnoxious prattle, he reached for the notebook on the table beside the cot. He lit the cooking-oil lamp and wrote down his dream.

Saloop dragged himself toward the light like some obese moth and put his head on the cot. Siri scratched it.

"You didn't happen to see a bear in the yard this morning, did you?" Siri asked.

As always, Saloop kept his secrets to himself. He'd neglected his duties. He'd been off romancing the bitch at the ice-works. He smelled the intruder when he got back, sure enough. It wasn't a scent he'd come across before. But it was something big and terrifying.

TRAVEL THE WORLD FOR $9.99

The first books in our most popular series in a new low price paperback edition

ITALY

DEATH OF AN ENGLISHMAN
MAGDALEN NABB
ISBN 978-1-61695-299-0

SLOVAKIA

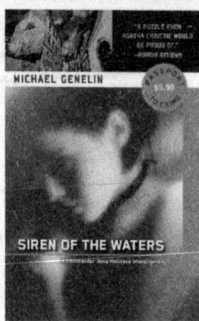

SIREN OF THE WATERS
MICHAEL GENELIN
ISBN 978-1-56947-585-0

WWII EUROPE

BILLY BOYLE
JAMES R. BENN
ISBN 978-1-61695-355-3

SOUTH AFRICA

RANDOM VIOLENCE
JASSY MACKENZIE
ISBN 978-1-61695-218-1

WWII BERLIN

ZOO STATION
DAVID DOWNING
ISBN 978-1-61695-348-5

PARIS

MURDER IN THE MARAIS
CARA BLACK
ISBN 978-1-56947-999-5

AUSTRALIA

THE DRAGON MAN
GARRY DISHER
ISBN 978-1-61695-448-2

LONDON, ENGLAND

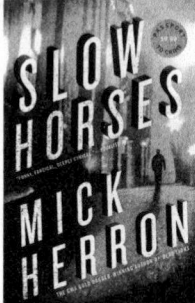

SLOW HORSES
MICK HERRON
ISBN 978-1-61695-416-1

PASSPORT $9.99 TO CRIME

BATH, ENGLAND

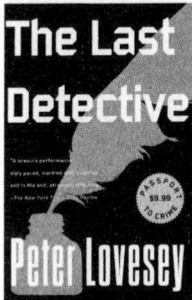

THE LAST DETECTIVE
PETER LOVESEY
ISBN 978-1-61695-081-1

AMSTERDAM

OUTSIDER IN AMSTERDAM
JANWILLEM VAN DE WETERING
ISBN 978-1-61695-300-3

HOLLYWOOD

CRASHED
TIMOTHY HALLINAN
ISBN 978-1-61695-276-1

SWEDEN

DETECTIVE INSPECTOR HUSS
HELENE TURSTEN
ISBN 978-1-61695-111-5

SOUTH KOREA

JADE LADY BURNING
MARTIN LIMÓN
ISBN 978-1-61695-090-3

BRAZIL

BLOOD OF THE WICKED
LEIGHTON GAGE
ISBN 978-1-61695-180-1

OTHER TITLES IN THE SOHO CRIME SERIES

Stephanie Barron
(Jane Austen's England)
*Jane and the Twelve Days
of Christmas*

Quentin Bates
(Iceland)
*Frozen Assets
Cold Comfort
Chilled to the Bone*

James R. Benn
(World War II Europe)
*Billy Boyle
The First Wave
Blood Alone
Evil for Evil
Rag & Bone
A Mortal Terror
Death's Door
A Blind Goddess
The Rest Is Silence*

Cara Black
(Paris, France)
*Murder in the Marais
Murder in Belleville
Murder in the Sentier
Murder in the Bastille
Murder in Clichy
Murder in Montmartre
Murder on the Ile Saint-Louis
Murder in the Rue de Paradis
Murder in the Latin Quarter
Murder in the Palais Royal
Murder in Passy
Murder at the Lanterne Rouge
Murder Below Montparnasse
Murder in Pigalle
Murder on the Champ de Mars*

Grace Brophy
(Italy)
*The Last Enemy
A Deadly Paradise*

Henry Chang
(Chinatown)
*Chinatown Beat
Year of the Dog
Red Jade
Death Money*

Barbara Cleverly
(England)
*The Last Kashmiri Rose
Strange Images of Death
The Blood Royal
Not My Blood*

Barbara Cleverly cont.
*A Spider in the Cup
Enter Pale Death*

Gary Corby
(Ancient Greece)
*The Pericles Commission
The Ionia Sanction
Sacred Games
The Marathon Conspiracy
Death Ex Machina*

Colin Cotterill
(Laos)
*The Coroner's Lunch
Thirty-Three Teeth
Disco for the Departed
Anarchy and Old Dogs
Curse of the Pogo Stick
The Merry Misogynist
Love Songs from a Shallow Grave
Slash and Burn
The Woman Who Wouldn't Die
The Six and a Half Deadly Sins*

Garry Disher
(Australia)
*The Dragon Man
Kittyhawk Down
Snapshot
Chain of Evidence
Blood Moon
Wyatt
Whispering Death
Port Vila Blues
Fallout
Hell to Pay*

David Downing
(World War II Germany)
*Zoo Station
Silesian Station
Stettin Station
Potsdam Station
Lehrter Station
Masaryk Station*

(World War I)
Jack of Spies

Leighton Gage
(Brazil)
*Blood of the Wicked
Buried Strangers
Dying Gasp
Every Bitter Thing
A Vine in the Blood
Perfect Hatred
The Ways of Evil Men*

Michael Genelin
(Slovakia)
*Siren of the Waters
Dark Dreams
The Magician's Accomplice
Requiem for a Gypsy*

Timothy Hallinan
(Thailand)
*The Fear Artist
For the Dead*

(Los Angeles)
*Crashed
Little Elvises
The Fame Thief
Herbie's Game*

Mette Ivie Harrison
(Mormon Utah)
The Bishop's Wife

Mick Herron
(England)
*Down Cemetery Road
The Last Voice You Hear
Reconstruction
Smoke and Whispers
Why We Die
Slow Horses
Dead Lions
Nobody Walks*

Lene Kaaberbøl & Agnete Friis
(Denmark)
*The Boy in the Suitcase
Invisible Murder
Death of a Nightingale*

Graeme Kent
(Solomon Islands)
*Devil-Devil
One Blood*

Heda Margolius Kovály
(1950s Prague)
Innocence

James Lilliefors
(Global Thrillers)
*Viral
The Leviathan Effect*

Martin Limón
(South Korea)
*Jade Lady Burning
Slicky Boys
Buddha's Money
The Door to Bitterness*

Martin Limón cont.
The Wandering Ghost
G.I. Bones
Mr. Kill
The Joy Brigade
Nightmare Range
The Iron Sickle

Ed Lin
(Taiwan)
Ghost Month

Peter Lovesey
(England)
The Circle
The Headhunters
False Inspector Dew
Rough Cider
On the Edge
The Reaper

(Bath, England)
The Last Detective
Diamond Solitaire
The Summons
Bloodhounds
Upon a Dark Night
The Vault
Diamond Dust
The House Sitter
The Secret Hangman
Skeleton Hill
Stagestruck
Cop to Corpse
The Tooth Tattoo
The Stone Wife

Jassy Mackenzie
(South Africa)
Random Violence
Stolen Lives
The Fallen
Pale Horses

Seichō Matsumoto
(Japan)
Inspector Imanishi Investigates

James McClure
(South Africa)
The Steam Pig
The Caterpillar Cop
The Gooseberry Fool
Snake
The Sunday Hangman
The Blood of an Englishman
The Artful Egg
The Song Dog

Magdalen Nabb
(Italy)
Death of an Englishman
Death of a Dutchman
Death in Springtime
Death in Autumn
The Marshal and the Madwoman
The Marshal and the Murderer
The Marshal's Own Case
The Marshal Makes His Report
The Marshal at the Villa Torrini
Property of Blood
Some Bitter Taste
The Innocent
Vita Nuova
The Monster of Florence

Fuminori Nakamura
(Japan)
The Thief
Evil and the Mask
Last Winter, We Parted

Stuart Neville
(Northern Ireland)
The Ghosts of Belfast
Collusion
Stolen Souls
The Final Silence
Ratlines

Eliot Pattison
(Tibet)
Prayer of the Dragon
The Lord of Death

Rebecca Pawel
(1930s Spain)
Death of a Nationalist
Law of Return
The Watcher in the Pine
The Summer Snow

Kwei Quartey
(Ghana)
Murder at Cape Three Points

Qiu Xiaolong
(China)
Death of a Red Heroine
A Loyal Character Dancer
When Red Is Black

John Straley
(Alaska)
The Woman Who Married a Bear
The Curious Eat Themselves
The Big Both Ways
Cold Storage, Alaska

Akimitsu Takagi
(Japan)
The Tattoo Murder Case
Honeymoon to Nowhere
The Informer

Helene Tursten
(Sweden)
Detective Inspector Huss
The Torso
The Glass Devil
Night Rounds
The Golden Calf
The Fire Dance
The Beige Man

Jan Merete Weiss
(Italy)
These Dark Things
A Few Drops of Blood

Janwillem van de Wetering
(Holland)
Outsider in Amsterdam
Tumbleweed
The Corpse on the Dike
Death of a Hawker
The Japanese Corpse
The Blond Baboon
The Maine Massacre
The Mind-Murders
The Streetbird
The Rattle-Rat
Hard Rain
Just a Corpse at Twilight
Hollow-Eyed Angel
The Perfidious Parrot
Amsterdam Cops: Collected Stories

Timothy Williams
(Guadeloupe)
Another Sun
The Honest Folk of Guadeloupe

(Italy)
Converging Parallels
The Puppeteer
Persona Non Grata
Black August
Big Italy

Jacqueline Winspear
(1920s England)
Maisie Dobbs
Birds of a Feather